Cave Baby

Written by

Julia Donaldson

Illustrated by

Emily Gravett

MACMILLAN CHILDREN'S BOOKS

Cave Baby's lucky – he lives inside a cave
With his mum (who's good at painting)
and his dad (who's very brave)

And a sabre-toothed tiger,
   a hyena and a hare
And a grey woolly mammoth, and a big brown bear.

Cave Baby's lonely. Nobody will play.
Dad is busy being brave. Mum says, "Keep away."

Everything is boring . . .
    Then suddenly it's not,
For in a corner of the cave he finds a brush and pot.

Spots on the hyena!

Stripes on the hare!

Stars on the tiger!

Squiggles on the bear!

Zigzags on the mammoth!

This is lots of fun . . .

But Mum and Dad are furious,
and say, "Look what he's done!"
Cave Mum fetches water. She mutters and she wipes.

No more spots and squiggles!

No more stars and stripes!

Cave Dad wags his finger.

"If you don't take care,
A mammoth's going to throw you to the big brown bear!"

Cave Baby's restless. He's feeling wide awake.
A long grey trunk comes sneaking in,
all wiggly like a snake.

"Where are you taking me?
    Where, tell me where?
Are you going to throw me to the big brown bear?"

Stripes in the forest! A tiger's lurking there. "Don't throw me to the tiger or

the big brown bear!"

Crashing in the bushes! A hare is leaping there. Maybe he's escaping from

the big brown bear!

A cackle in the bracken! A hyena's laughing there.

Has he heard a joke about the big brown bear?

A cave in the hillside! "I wonder who lives there?
I hope it's not . . . Don't let it be . . . the big brown bear!"

The cave is bright with moonlight. The walls are plain and bare.
Snoring in the shadows! Someone's sleeping there.
Cave Baby's worried. He doesn't understand . . .
Until the woolly mammoth pops a paintbrush in his hand.

A five-legged tiger!

A long curly hare!

Horns on a hyena!

A beard on a bear!

A moustache on a mammoth!

This is lots of fun!

Then the mammoth wakes his family
And says, "Look what he's done!"

And they rollick and they frolic, they trumpet and they crash,
They wade into the water. They roll and romp and splash.

They shake the baby by the hand, then lift their trunks and wave
As the mammoth picks him up again and takes him to his cave.

Cave Baby's happy. He's fast asleep in bed.
He dreams about a tiger with stripes of pink and red,
And a grass-green hyena, and a sky-blue hare,
And a moon-yellow mammoth . . . and a small brown bear.

For Esther Gabriela – J.D.

For Dad & V.W. – E.G.

First published 2010 by Macmillan Children's Books
This edition published 2011 by Macmillan Children's Books
a division of Macmillan Publishers Limited
20 New Wharf Road, London N1 9RR
Basingstoke and Oxford
Associated companies throughout the world
www.panmacmillan.com

ISBN: 978-1-5098-0123-7

Text copyright © Julia Donaldson 2010
Illustrations copyright © Emily Gravett 2010
Moral rights asserted.

3 5 7 9 8 6 4 2

A CIP catalogue record for this book is available from the British Library.

Printed in China